Bellerose

WALT DISNEY PRODUCTIONS
presents

Mickey's Christmas Carol

Based on *A Christmas Carol* by Charles Dickens

Featuring Mickey Mouse as Bob Cratchit

Random House 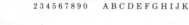 New York

Book Club Edition

Copyright © 1982 by Walt Disney Productions. All rights reserved
under International and Pan-American Copyright Conventions.
Published in the United States by Random House, Inc., New
York, and simultaneously in Canada by Random House of Canada
Limited, Toronto. ISBN: 0-394-85615-5 Manufactured in the
United States of America
2 3 4 5 6 7 8 9 0   A B C D E F G H I J K

On the day before Christmas, Ebenezer
Scrooge walked into his counting house
and surprised his clerk at the stove.

"What do you think you are doing,
Bob Cratchit?" barked Scrooge.

"J-just adding some coal to the stove,"
said Cratchit. "It's so cold in here that
the ink froze!"

"You can warm the ink in your hands," said Scrooge. "Now quit wasting my coal and get back to work!"

"Yes, sir. And speaking of work, sir, tomorrow is Christmas. May I please have the day off?" asked Cratchit.

"Bah! Oh, I suppose so," said Scrooge. "But you won't get any pay."

"No, sir. Thank you, sir!" said Cratchit.

Scrooge and Cratchit
settled down to work.

But suddenly the door
burst open.

In came Scrooge's nephew,
Fred.

"Merry Christmas, everyone!"
Fred called.

"What do YOU want?" asked Scrooge.
"I've come to give you a wreath and
invite you to Christmas dinner," said Fred.
"Families should be together at Christmas."

"Bah, humbug!" said
Scrooge. "I am not
interested in family
or Christmas. Now
go away. I'm busy!"

"But Uncle," said
Fred, "you will miss
a wonderful dinner.
We're going to have
roast goose with
chestnut dressing . . .

plum pudding with
lemon sauce . . .
candied fruits with
spiced sugar cakes. . . .
Now, won't you come?"

"Are you daft, man?" said Scrooge.
"You know I can't eat that stuff!"

"Come if you change your mind," said Fred,
and he handed the wreath to his uncle.

"Here, I don't want this thing!" said
Scrooge.

But Fred was already out the door.

"Bah, humbug!" said
Scrooge.

He said it all day.

And he was still
saying it when he
left work that night.

Scrooge spent Christmas Eve at home in front of the fire.

He was just dozing off when he heard the sound of chains.

Then a voice moaned, "Scroo-o-o-ge!"

"Who's there?" asked Scrooge.

There stood the ghost of
Scrooge's dead partner,
Jacob Marley.

"I have a message for
you, Scrooge," said Marley.
"You know how
I used to steal
from widows and
cheat the poor?"

"Yes, and all in the same day!"
said Scrooge.

"It was wrong of me," said Marley.
"Now I am being punished."

"I must drag around these heavy chains and cash boxes—forever," said Marley. "And the same thing will happen to you, Ebenezer Scrooge!"

Scrooge gasped.

"No, no! Help me, Jacob!" he begged.

"Tonight you will be visited by three spirits. Do what they say—or your chains will be heavier than mine," said Marley.

Then old Marley
disappeared through
the door.
   "Farewell-l-l-l,"
he called.

"No, wait, Jacob!"
cried Scrooge. "Come
back. Tell me more!"
But the ghost of
Marley was gone.

At bedtime Scrooge looked nervously
around, but there was no one to be seen.
"Spirits, eh?" he said. "Bah, humbug!"

Scrooge was soon fast asleep.
But in the middle of the night
a soft "ding, ding, ding" woke him up.
He peeked between the bed curtains.
Somebody was tapping the bell on
his alarm clock!
"Wake up, wake up!" said the stranger.
"Who are you?" asked Scrooge.

"I am the Ghost of Christmas Past," said the stranger.

He hopped onto Scrooge's hand.

"Hold on to me— but not too tight," he said. "We're going to visit your past."

The spirit opened his umbrella and —WHOOSH!—he and Scrooge rose to the sky.

Scrooge and the spirit
flew high over the rooftops.
Scrooge was too scared
to look.

The spirit
and Scrooge
landed in
front of a
brightly lit
window.

"Spirit, I know this place!" said Scrooge.
"It's the warehouse where I worked as a lad.
What good times I had here with my friends!"
The spirit wiped snow off the windowpane,
and Scrooge looked in at a Christmas party.

Under the mistletoe a lovely young lady
danced with a shy young man.

"Why, it's Isabel and me!" said Scrooge.
He watched the young lady and sighed.
"How I once loved her," he said.

"Until you learned to love
money more!" said the spirit.

Scrooge's eyes filled with tears.

"All my old friends . . . they're all lost
to me now," he said sadly.

"That's the way you wanted it, you know,"
said the spirit.

"Oh, Spirit, please take me home," cried
Scrooge. "I can't bear to remember any more."

And the next thing he knew, he was back
in his bed, and his alarm clock was ringing.

Scrooge opened the bed curtains.
There stood a giant!
"Who are you?" cried Scrooge as
the giant's hand reached for him.

The giant picked up Scrooge and said,
"I am the Ghost of Christmas Present.
I'm taking you to meet some people
with kindness in their hearts—even for
a mean old miser like you."

And he popped Scrooge
into his pocket.

The giant walked through the streets
until he reached a poor part of town.

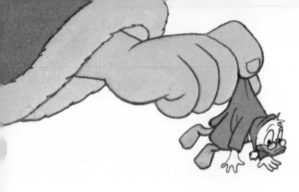

The giant set
Scrooge down
in front of
a shabby house.

It was the home of Bob Cratchit,
Scrooge's underpaid clerk.

Bob and his merry children
were trimming a tree.

It was time for
Christmas dinner.
"Where is Tiny Tim?"
said Cratchit.
"Coming, Father!"
called the little boy
as he limped down
the stairs.

Bob picked up his
lame son and carried
him to the table.
"My, what a feast!"
said Tiny Tim.

And it WAS a feast for the Cratchits.
But there really wasn't much food.

"Let's drink a toast to Mr. Scrooge," said Tiny Tim. "We owe our wonderful dinner to him."

Scrooge was touched.

"There's a kind lad," he said.

"But the boy looks so sickly," Scrooge said. "Tell me, Spirit, what is wrong with him?"

"Much, I'm afraid," said the giant.

"What will happen to Tim?" asked Scrooge.
There was no answer.
Scrooge turned around.
The giant was gone, and in his place stood the Ghost of Christmas Future.

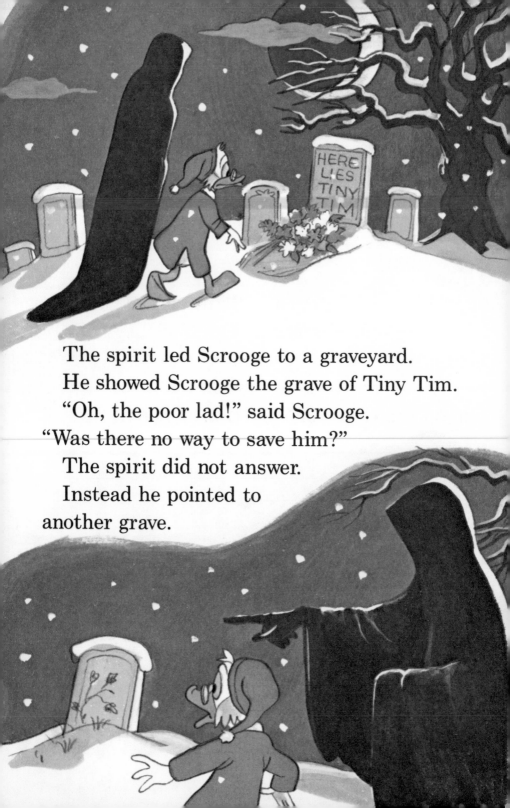

The spirit led Scrooge to a graveyard.
He showed Scrooge the grave of Tiny Tim.
"Oh, the poor lad!" said Scrooge.
"Was there no way to save him?"
The spirit did not answer.
Instead he pointed to
another grave.

With fear in his heart, Scrooge walked up
to the grave.

Weeds grew all over it.

No one cared about the person buried there.

Scrooge read the headstone and gasped.

The grave was his own!

Scrooge ran from his grave in terror.
"Spirit, tell me it's not too late!"
he cried. "Tell me I still have time to
change. I'll change. I promise I'll change.
I'll help Tiny Tim. Things will be better!"

Suddenly Scrooge tripped on a tree root
and tumbled down,

              down,

                    down . . .

. . . and landed with a bump on a hard floor.
Dazed, Scrooge looked around.

He was in his own bedroom!
And daylight was coming in the window.

Scrooge ran to the window and
threw it open.

He could hear church bells ringing.

"It's Christmas morning!" he cried.
"It's not too late! The spirits gave me
another chance!"

"I know just what
I'll do," Scrooge said.

He dressed in a hurry.

Then he ran out of the house
and rushed down the street.

"Pennies for the poor?" asked two men.
They were collecting for charity.

"Pennies? You need gold!" cried Scrooge.
And he dropped some gold coins into
their cup.

Then he danced off
down the street.

Scrooge found a toy shop and bought
a big bag of toys.

"Won't they be surprised!" he said.
"I can't wait to see their faces!"

Scrooge saw his nephew driving by.
"Merry Christmas, Fred!" he called.
Fred stopped with a jolt.
"Uncle Scrooge!" he said in surprise.

"I'm looking forward to your delicious
Christmas dinner," said Scrooge.
"You mean you're coming?" asked Fred.
"Of course!" said Scrooge.

Scrooge walked through the town, calling
"Merry Christmas" to everyone he saw.

Finally he reached a shabby home.
He stopped and knocked on the door.

"Merry Christmas, Cratchit!" said Scrooge
as his surprised clerk opened the door.
"I've brought some things for the children."

And he gave them the most wonderful toys
they had ever seen.

"And for you, Cratchit," said Scrooge, "a raise. A big one!"

"Oh, thank you, sir," said Cratchit, and he and his wife danced for joy.

Scrooge had a merry visit with the family.
He ate and drank and even played with
the children.

"A toast to all the Cratchits!" said Scrooge.

And Tiny Tim added, "And God bless us . . .
every one!"